OUT OF THE DARK

Written by Tennant Redbank
Based on the screenplay written by Eddy Kitsis & Adam Horowitz
Based on characters created by Steven Lisberger and Bonnie MacBird
Executive Producer Donald Kushner
Produced by Sean Bailey, Jeffrey Silver, Steven Lisberger
Directed by Joseph Kosinski

DISNEP PRESS
NEW YORK

Printed in the United States of America

First Edition
1 3 5 7 9 10 8 6 4 2
G658-7729-4-10244

Library of Congress Catalog Card Number on file.
ISBN 978-1-4231-3150-2

Visit Disneybooks.com

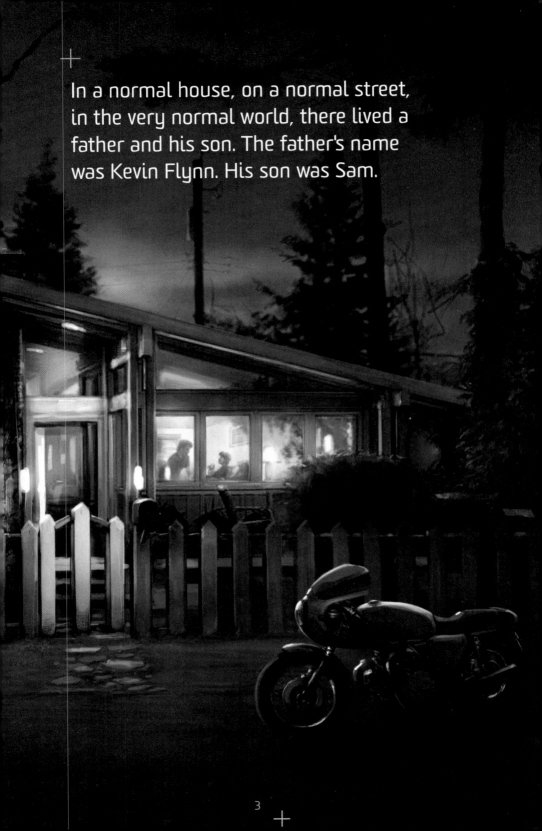

In a normal house, on a normal street, in the very normal world, there lived a father and his son. The father's name was Kevin Flynn. His son was Sam.

Kevin was a busy man, but he always made time for his son. At night, he told Sam fantastical bedtime stories about an amazing digital universe.

"I kept dreaming of a world I thought I'd never see," Flynn said to Sam one evening as he tucked him under the covers. "Then one day . . ."

"You got in," Sam finished. In this story, his dad lived *inside* the computer.

"That's right," Flynn said, nodding. He checked his watch. "Look at that. Way past bedtime." He stood up.

"Dad, don't go to work tonight," Sam begged.

But Flynn left anyway. He had to.

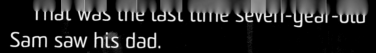

That was the last time seven-year-old Sam saw his dad.

Years passed, and Sam grew up. He was smart, like his dad. But he was also sad. He missed his father.

Then one night, Flynn's partner, Alan Bradley, visited Sam. He told him he received a message from Sam's dad.

The message had come from the office at Flynn's arcade. No one had been there for twenty years.

Sam decided to check it out. When he walked into the dusty arcade, it looked the same as it had years ago. He decided to play one round of his father's favorite game, Tron. But then he noticed something. There was a secret door behind the game! He slipped inside.

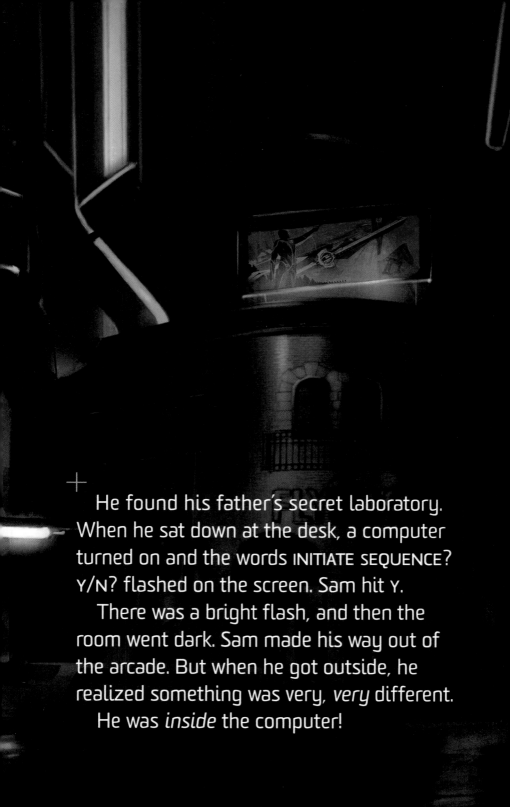

He found his father's secret laboratory.
When he sat down at the desk, a computer
turned on and the words INITIATE SEQUENCE?
Y/N? flashed on the screen. Sam hit Y.

There was a bright flash, and then the
room went dark. Sam made his way out of
the arcade. But when he got outside, he
realized something was very, *very* different.

He was *inside* the computer!

Sam quickly discovered that this world was full of beings called programs that looked human. But they were made up of computer code. The world was called the Grid, and it was ruled by someone named Clu.

Clu liked to have the programs compete in games against each other. Sam had to play. Luckily, he was very good!

When Clu saw how good Sam was at the games, he grew suspicious. He brought him to his ship and discovered the truth—Sam was human!

This was not good for Clu. He couldn't have a human on the Grid. So he challenged Sam to the most dangerous game of all—a Light Cycle race.

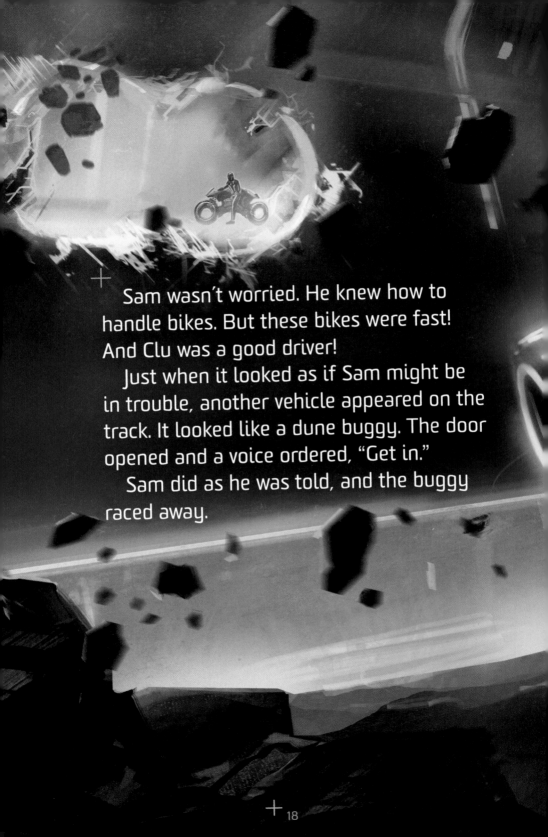

Sam wasn't worried. He knew how to handle bikes. But these bikes were fast! And Clu was a good driver!

Just when it looked as if Sam might be in trouble, another vehicle appeared on the track. It looked like a dune buggy. The door opened and a voice ordered, "Get in."

Sam did as he was told, and the buggy raced away.

When they were safely away from the track, the driver turned to Sam. "I'm Quorra," she said, lifting her visor.

Sam was surprised. "Where are you taking me?" he asked.

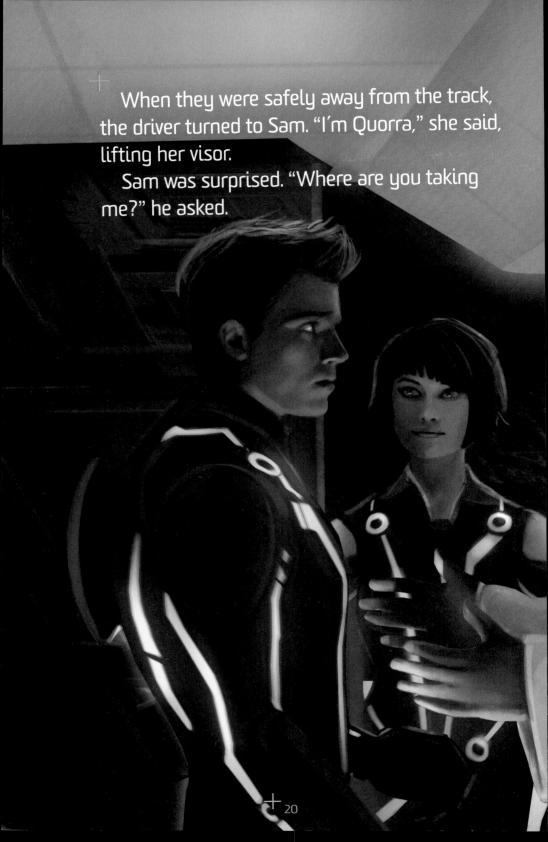

"Patience, Sam Flynn. All your questions will be answered soon," she said.

A while later she pulled into a hidden cave entrance. Inside the hideaway, Sam got a surprise. His father was there!

Sam couldn't believe it. All those years, his father had been trapped in this world. Now they could be together again! They just had to get to the Portal that would take them back to the real world.

But when Sam told him they should go, his father refused. "Sometimes life has a way of moving you past things like wants and hopes," Kevin said.

There was no way Sam was going to take no for an answer, though. He'd find a way out, and then come back for his dad.

"There's someone I once knew," Quorra told him when he decided to go. "A program named Zuse." She gave him directions to where Sam could find Zuse.

Sam didn't waste any time. He hopped on his father's old Light Cycle and headed into the heart of the Grid.

He was going to the End of Line Club. Hopefully, there he'd find Zuse—and a way out of this world.

It took Sam only a few minutes to find the mysterious Zuse. He wore all white and had pale skin and white hair. In his hand he carried a white cane that he twirled with glee.

"I need to get to the Portal," Sam told the man.

"It's quite the journey," Zuse replied. But he agreed to help Sam.

Suddenly, Clu's army—the Black Guard—
burst into the room. Zuse had been lying!
He didn't want to help Sam—he wanted to

Sam began to fight. But he was outnumbered. Then, out of the corner of his eye, he saw Quorra. She'd come to help!

Quorra hadn't come alone, though.
Kevin Flynn appeared, and with his help,
they escaped from the End of Line Club.
But the danger wasn't over. Now that
Kevin had shown his face on the Grid,
Clu would be after him. They needed to
find a way home . . . soon.

9